A LION AT A COCKTAIL PARTY

Michael Hogan

GALLIMAUFRY

Arlington

1978

ACKNOWLEDGMENTS

Grateful acknowledgment is made to the following magazines in which some of these prose pieces first appeared: *Iowa Review*, *Madrona*, *The Chowder Review*, *New Letters*, *Gallimaufry*, and *Snakeroots*.

''The Virgin of San Loc'' and ''The Tiger'' first appeared in issues #40 and #42 of *kayak*, and the author wishes to particularly thank George Hitchcock, the editor of that magazine, whose encouragement and criticism proved invaluable.

''The Tour'' first appeared in *If You Ever Get There, Think of Me*, copyright © 1975 by Michael Hogan. Permission to reprint from Emerald City Press is gratefully acknowledged.

Some of these pieces were previously published in *April 1976*, a sound recording of a reading by the author, published by Cold Mountain Press and copyright © 1975, 1976 by Michael Hogan.

The author is particularly grateful to the Literature Program of the National Endowment for the Arts, whose timely assistance gave him (quite literally) the freedom to write this book.

Published by:
GALLIMAUFRY
P.O. Box 32364
Calvert Street Station
Washington, D.C. 20001

CONTENTS

IV : GOLDEN

A LION AT A COCKTAIL PARTY

We become aware of the void as we fill it.
The void terrifies us, and yet our eyes open wider.
—Antonio Porchia

I : RESISTANCE

The Tiger

You are in an elevator. The doors close. Inside: soft light, two passengers. A man with a briefcase. A cleaning woman. The cleaning woman's hair is in curlers, she is old. On the back wall: a print of a painting by Gauguin. Lush tropical plants with thick green stems, oversized red blooms swirling away from a tiger hidden deep in Tahitian undergrowth. Beneath the panel on the right side is a notice:

IN CASE OF A MALFUNCTION OF THE CABLES CAUSING THIS ELEVATOR TO FALL SUDDENLY TO THE BOTTOM, IT IS ESSENTIAL THAT YOU KEEP THE FOLLOWING IN MIND:

1. It is absolutely imperative that no part of your body is touching the floor upon impact.

2. If this elevator is equipped with side rails, then jump and cling desperately to the rails.

3. If this elevator is not equipped with side rails, use your luggage to cushion the impact.

You are in an elevator and it is climbing steadily toward the top. There is a stop on the twelfth floor for the man with the briefcase. Another, on the thirtieth for the cleaning lady. But you are going on. Half-remembered stories of elevators crashing, burning buildings, radarless planes screaming into skyscrapers are buried somewhere back of your next appointment, behind a birthday gift for your son, the house payment. And suddenly, at the thirty-fifth floor, the elevator slows for a stop. It shudders briefly. It hands in space suspended by fraying cables. It shudders again as the cable snaps, and smoke and the smell of grease and rubber fill the car as the brakes fight frantically to hold. And then it plunges down, and there is no sound but the rush of your blood and the high scream that escapes like a whistle. And the floor of the elevator is leaping out from beneath you as you remember:

It is essential . . . absolutely imperative in
case of malfunction . . . no part of your

body touching the floor upon impact. If
this elevator is equipped with side rails . . .
cling desperately . . . if this elevator is not
equipped with side rails, use your luggage to
cushion the impact . . .

But there are no side rails and you have no luggage. So you try to jump but you cannot. Your feet are planted in steel and concrete. *They* cling desperately. Red flowers grow in your brain. An educated man, at home in the city. You met your obligations, your life was well-planned and orderly. Surely there is some mistake. There should have been suitcases. Handles. There should have been time to prepare before the green stems snapping, before the Tahitian blossoms, red and screaming, and you alone with the tiger. The brief yellow gleam of his eyes.

Mrs. Entity and the Vacuum Cleaner

Mrs. Entity had substance. Her husband, a thin, balding man, wanted mostly to be left alone. He seldom had his wish. As a consequence he leaked substance like a sieve.

"You leak substance like a sieve," his wife told him.

"More like a gravy strainer," he replied. "And you are there mopping me up with bread, getting fatter every day. I'm disappearing. There's little left of me but a greasy stain or an occasional lump of flour."

Mrs. Entity licked her chops. She had a substantial interest in the substance of the conversation. "Leave me alone," said her husband. "Let me read a book without these interruptions." Mrs. Entity began running the vacuum cleaner.

"Stop that infernal racket!" shouted the husband, leaking substance all over the carpet.

Finally she stopped. But not until the carpet was clean as an altar boy's surplice. And later, when she emptied the bag, there was a greasy stain and one or two lumps substantially like flour.

A Believer in Stones

I have a friend who believes that stones are alive. "Seeing is believing," he says. "After every rainstorm there are as many new stones as tadpoles. It is clear they give birth in damp weather."

This is not a common belief, but it has a rational foundation. If he lived in California my friend would have many followers. He'd be the pastor of the First Stone Church. They would all worship the moon, prime mover of stones, under whose benevolent gaze they propagate each monsoon season.

Being a believer in stones causes a few difficulties, but there are compensations. For example, while my friend's conversations are rather one-sided, he saves drastically on food bills.

"Would you care for some more zucchini, Mr. Paleolithic? No? How about you, Ms. Pre-Cambrian?"

They never answer. Sometimes after dinner one or two roll off the table. They fall asleep in the moonlight which shines through the kitchen window. But this never causes any problems for my friend. He is very careful to get the stones outside before the rains come.

Resistance

Sunday morning and the boy walks to church, self-contained and insular as a tank. His corduroys whistle, his Buster Browns squeak, his face gleams like a Simonized Chevy. The father tips a straw hat to some ladies passing. The mother's Daily Missal is crammed like a country churchyard with *In Memoriams*. The sister is fresh, perfect as an Easter lily or the structure of a DNA molecule.

Between the sidewalk and the street is a strip of grass. It extends along the length of the walk but is cut unevenly, being mowed in sections at different times by homeowners whose parcels it borders. Here the grass is dry, powdery as plutonium. There it is green, smooth and lush as the felt on a pool table. Or here it is high the way rye grass is in a vacant lot.

The boy observes these things. He sees the ants cluster around a popsickle stick, how they bunch and spread outward like a mixture in a centrifuge. He watches the bees flowing like electrons among the clover. Then his mother turns abruptly. "Would you *please* walk on the sidewalk like a *normal* person!"

He walks on the sidewalk.

They move on past the rectory and the brown house on the corner, headed toward the church. The boy follows close behind, listening to his mother's spiked heels striking the pavement. Suddenly, he raises his right arm, thrusting it out like a spear. "Seig Heil!", he says, stopping, bringing the heels of his Buster Browns together. Then he follows on, self-contained and insular as a tank.

Case History

"I simply carry out instructions," said the Sergeant. If I made policy that would be a different story. But the rules have been established by the others and I have no choice but to enforce them."

"I demand to see my child!" insisted the mother.

"And I've told you that's quite impossible at this time. The rules provide that during the first thirty days of isolation and orientation the child shall not be allowed visitors. There can be no exceptions to that policy."

They had taken her child while she was in jail and placed him in the children's colony. Custody was impossible until the trial and maybe not even then if things did not go well.

"How do I know my child is even in there?" she asked.

"Come, come, madam, you're wasting my time. Why would you be here if he was not?"

"Well, then, how do I know he's okay? That he's in good health?"

"You have my word for that," the Sergeant replied.

When the thirty day period finally expired, the woman returned. She met the Sergeant at the front gate. "Excuse me," she apologized. "My son? May I see him now?"

"Of course! Of course! No problem!" replied the Sergeant.

But several minutes passed and the woman was very tired. She stretched out on the bench in front of the dormitory. An hour passed. By the time the Sergeant returned, she was sleeping soundly.

"Wake up, madam! Wake up!" he said, shaking her roughly. "Here is your child!"

She awoke and looked wildly around her. "No! No!" she screamed. "I won't let you do that to me again!" Then she ran out of the colony and down the roadway.

The child ran after her crying. "Please, mother, please!" But soon the child was out of breath. He gave up chasing her. He returned to the colony and became strangely quiet.

The welfare report says that he was comfortable there and became friendly with the Sergeant. It also says that, after the first two years, most of the bad dreams did not recur.

Hardly Convivial

See the children. They are all collecting boxes. This little boy has six boxes. He's already forgotten colors do not come without light. Color is wax. Light comes out of a tube. Everything is properly contained.

His sister has ten boxes. Hardly enough for her. But when she gets just twelve boxes she will leave home. She will marry. She'll always regret not getting extra boxes. She'll be unhappy. This is quite natural. She'll tell the neighbors, ''My daughter will not get cheated out of the boxes coming to her.''

Can you imagine not needing any boxes? Would you let a man without boxes marry your sister? Then don't be ridiculous. Not having boxes is un-American. Worse. Even Communists have boxes. What you are proposing is completely outrageous. Fortunately for you we are going inside our boxes. We cannot hear you in there.

A Place for Everything

We do not like the maze in the garden, because it too closely resembles the maze in the brain.
—T.S. Eliot

Buzzer Martin believed that certain things were very important even though at face value they might not seem so to most people. For example, he felt that order was very important. Absence of order is chaos. In society, anarchy. In music, disharmony. In dress, slovenliness, an indication of disorder in the mind.

Buzzer was a man who liked everything in its place. In his top bureau drawer, for example, he kept his socks. The white ones on the right, the colored ones on the left. In the back of the top drawer were handkerchiefs.

In the middle drawer he kept t-shirts, shorts (but not swim trunks or tennis shorts) and three pairs of work pants. This arrangement was convenient because he always woke early, putting on his socks, underclothes and pants in the dark to avoid waking his wife.

He would get breakfast ready, go into the bedroom, and then wake her with a kiss. It was something she neither liked nor disliked. She did not need breakfast in bed, but it made him feel good to kiss her there, to see her heavy-lidded and satiated when he left for work. It made him feel he was taking good care of her, and she never had the heart to deny him this.

In fact, she had never been completely happy since the day she married Buzzer. There were many things she had to do which other wives did not. And each of these things had to be done perfectly. For example, when she made the bed she had to use two fresh sheets each morning. Buzzer liked the smell of fresh sheets. The bottom sheet had to lap over the bottom of the mattress and be double-folded so that it would not be kicked out at night. The top sheet must then be tucked, and folded at the head of the bed precisely twice the width of the hem. Clean pillow cases were mandatory each day and—in addition to all this—the mattress must be aired and turned every other day.

Buzzer once flew into a rage when his wife lost a fingernail turning a mattress and left a small bloodstain on the wallpaper near the headboard. So, there was a great deal of anxiety associated with Mrs. Martin's household chores which was foreign to other women.

Buzzer hated dirt of any kind. He hated insects, unusual odors, anything not freshly laundered and neatly pressed. He wanted the bedroom antiseptic as a NASA lab and his wife was, quite frankly, afraid to let him down. Yet, as much as anything else, it was this very fear, this anxiety, which caused all the trouble.

On the afternoon in question, after ironing all the boxer shorts and t-shirts, Mrs. Martin had started folding socks. But a glance at the clock on the kitchen wall indicated it was almost four o'clock and time to get the dinner ready. So, she picked up the bundle of ironing, placed it in the top dresser drawer in the bedroom, then returned to the kitchen and began preparing dinner. She intended to straighten up the clothes after the dinner dishes were cleaned.

But, one thing led to another. After dinner there was the garbage to take out, the pots and pans to be cleaned, splashes of grease to be sponged off the wall, the floor to be mopped, things to be put up in the cabinets. By the time she had finished all this and had taken her bath, she was too exhausted to do anything but crawl into bed.

There is some speculation that she and Buzzer made love that night and there is no reason to presume this is not true. Buzzer surely felt content, secure, and amorous with a good dinner inside him, a clean house around him, fresh sheets touching his skin and—to all appearances, at least—everything in perfect order.

At any rate, he awoke the next morning and did exactly ten pushups, twenty deep kneebends, and touched his toes ten times. He walked over to the bureau and opened the top drawer.

At Buzzer's trial the wrappings from all six packages were introduced. One for each of the limbs, one for the trunk, and one for the head. The coroner said that the limbs and the head had been neatly severed by a buzz saw, the blood drained, and each section double-wrapped in aluminum foil then placed into a Hefty bag before being put in the freezer.

It was also the coroner who stated that evidence from the largest package indicated recent sexual intercourse. However, it was not clearly established if this had occurred on the night previously mentioned, or the next day when all but one of the packages were carefully placed in the freezer.

What My Sister Told Me

She said, "You know, a lot of people think that when you have a dream that you're falling, if you don't wake up before you hit the ground, you'll be dead."

"I've heard that was true."

"Well, the other night," she continued, "I tested it. I dreamed that I was falling and, instead of listening to the voice which said 'Wake up!', I continued to sleep."

"What happened next?" I asked.

"You'll have to discover that for yourself. But it's apparent that I'm not dead."

Indeed. Far from being dead she was more vital than I had ever seen her. Her smile was alarmingly seductive.

That night I fell asleep. I dreamed that I was falling. I ignored the voice inside me which told me to waken.

Ever since then, for no apparent reason, I smile at peolpe passing in the street. Many stop and tell me: "Do you know that you have a very seductive smile?" If they are quite extraordinary people, I tell them the secret. The others I take into the bushes. Have them remove their clothes. Send them home crying to their mothers.

The Furnace

Bored by life in the basement, a furnace climbs the stairs and enters the living room. It begins watching t.v. After an hour or so it gets up and walks outside. It heads toward the city where it devours a used car lot, a record company, and the Coca Cola Bottling plant of Berkeley, California.

The furnace returns home in time for the six o'clock news. When the news is over, the furnace devours the wife and children. Then it puffs away in an old easy chair. But the heat from the furnace sets fire to the house. The furnace eats the television set and leaves.

An old drunk reports these occurances to the police. Then he discovers the Police Commissioner himself is a furnace, as is the Mayor, the Chairman of the School Board. They are looking for more combustible things. They build a detoxification center for the drunk. They build housing projects for the poor. They build schools.

Then all the drunks turn into furnaces, all the poor people, the children. Some start eating each other. Others are looking for more combustible things. There are one or two instances of resistance. But they appear doomed to fail. Economists have proven that an increase in furnaces raises the Gross National Product.

Applied Science

"What did you say your name was?" he asked, putting another culture onto the slide.

"I didn't say," she smiled.

Already ten people have died. They think it could be the swine flu or a similar strain of virus. No one is certain.

"We can rule out bacteria," he concluded, removing the slide.

"Mary," she smiled. "My name is Mary Hennessy."

A dozen people have died. All of them previously attended a Legion convention. Public health employees work around the clock, are hopeful it's a known virus.

"There's a possibility it's not a virus at all," she said. "Could be a chemical introduced through the food."

"I have a motel room less than a block away," he told her.

Seventeen people have died. A virus has yet to be isolated. A toxin cannot be ruled out.

"Please, please, please!" she cried.

Twenty-five people have died. They are hoping the latest autopsies produce more promising results.

"Was it good for you?" he asked.

"Liver tissue," she said, "would probably be most revealing."

II : GREAT-GRANDMOTHER'S EYES

The Tour

Behind the walls it is not like anything we had imagined. There are men in brown uniforms who direct traffic with walkie-talkies. Their conversation is in code and quite esoteric.

There are also men in blue uniforms. These are the ones being directed. They are, for the most part, expressionless, although here and there is a sullen one, a happy one, another who appears high on drugs.

The guard towers are manned by those in brown uniforms who were long ago bored with everything below. They have literally risen above their peers. We suspect they are discussing the metaphysical implications of their being where they are: high above both the traffic and those directing it; able to see clearly the saffron roof of the courthouse a quarter mile away.

We wonder what is happening here. The answers we get are fragmented or circular. Some of those in brown uniforms carry rhetoric to their work as a hobo carries garlic pearls to season his stew. Those in the blue uniforms carry guilt like ticks under their skin.

Last night it was reported the men in brown uniforms bought machineguns and installed them in the towers. Some of them look grim. Today, walking across the compound, those in the blue uniforms are laughing, jostling one another. The men in the guard towers have concluded their discussion. They are squinting through narrow sights.

Death Row

When the latest Supreme Court decision was handed down the Warden spoke to the condemned prisoners.

"The Court decided that the death penalty was constitutional. It's reasoning is infallible. I trust you'll accept it as a product of enlightened reasoning."

"What was the reasoning, Warden?" asked John Henry.

"Well, son," the Warden replied, "it was that the murderer should himself be the object of murder. It goes back to our Judaic-Christian heritage. An eye for an eye, etcetera. A philosophy ingrained in our people and accepted by the Founding Fathers. The logic is infallible. The instrument of murder must himself be murdered. Retributive justice."

"I see," said John Henry, reaching through the bars and strangling the Warden on the spot.

"John Henry!" shouted Calvin Lee. "What the fuck you gone and done, brother. You a goddam Muslim!"

"When in Rome," said John Henry, releasing the limp body, "one should try to see the merit of infallible logic."

"Wa salaam aliekem," said Calvin Lee.

"Amen," said John Henry.

The Speaking Cross

The Maya of Quintana Roo listen to the cross whenever it speaks. Sometimes its words can be interpreted in more than one fashion but that is the way with speaking crosses.

One day it told them: ''Be grateful for the rain.''

They took this to mean that the monsoon would come late and be of brief duration. They dug pits and lined them with rocks to conserve the small amount of water which would come. This interpretation was entirely speculative.

But, in fact, the rains did come late that year and only briefly. The pits saved the Maya from dying of thirst.

Also, that same year, white men invaded the village of Santa Cruz in the territory of Quintana Roo. They destroyed the cross. They exposed the pit beneath the sacred tree where an Indian ventriloquist was hidden. They thought the Indians would be completely demoralized. But, as soon as the white men withdrew to their camp for the night, the Indians raised another speaking cross.

No sooner was it erected than it told them: ''Trust to your faith.''

They took this to mean that they were a part of god. God was in them and they were in god. They had nothing to fear from the white man. This interpretation was entirely speculative.

But, in fact, the white man could not be bothered with such simple people, living in the jungle, talking to fradulent crosses. There were more important things to be done.

So the white men headed north where their priests converted tribes which had no silly artifacts. They erected crosses with a dead white man upon them. And they built churches. They built churches. They built churches. And the tribes in the north died out in five generations.

The Maya of Quintana Roo listen to the cross when it speaks. Sometimes its words can be interpreted in more than one fashion, but that is the way with speaking crosses.

At the Used Car Lot with a Friend

If the pen is an extension of the voice, then we are using forests for lungs. Words whisper in the leaves. And, if the automobile is an extension of our legs, it's not unusual to be choking on the smoke of our footsteps.

It's clear war's an extension of rape. The man below, who knows how the ladder works, pulls the rope. Rungs multiply, the ladder rises to many times the original length. This is called escalation. It is both phallic and democratic. The rapist makes us his accomplices.

It is obvious when years are extensions of days we begin living beyond our means. Our lives become those of our children or grandchildren. This is called progress. We avoid slipping back at all costs.

Prisons are extensions of locks. States, of street corner gangs. If their jackets don't have the right patch, we cut off their balls with a straight razor. This is sometimes called property rights. It is also referred to as territorial demands.

Extension slows when we see we're connected. And that connection preceeds rights and demands and survives them. The moon doesn't care to be Venus or Mercury. It moves the tides and is moved. And the saguaro has no desire to be a cactus wren and fly outside itself. It lives both inside and out.

I know you are not a saguaro. It is apparent you are not the moon. Certainly this goes against centuries of conditioning. But think about it. Do you really need a second car?

The Gift

Every day the boy would go down to the beach. He pretended that all the land as far as he could see belonged to him alone.

Early in the morning the beach would be empty except for the old man. He did not consider the old man a trespasser. The old man seemed a part of the beach as the starfish was a part, or the ''Give A Hoot, Don't Pollute'' sign near the boardwalk, or as the seashells were a part.

The boy pretended that all the ocean within sight belonged to him as well. When a tanker would pass close to the horizon throwing smoke like a shadow, ragged and ugly as a sand shark, the boy would yell. He would run up and down the beach waving his arms, warning the ship to keep moving, that it was in a forbidden area. The ship would take its time but gradually it would leave and the boy would look to the old man. The old man would wink. Sometimes he would say to himself quietly, ''That's my boy!''

The old man was playing a game, too. He was pretending that this beach and the ocean by it were parts of a world which he had given to the boy. Every morning he would come to the beach to watch how the boy handled the gift. Some day the flowing grasslands to the south and the mountains to the north would be his as well. He also knew that a time would come when the boy would give it all away to someone else. But this did not worry him. Nor did he and the boy ever speak of it.

Great-Grandmother's Eyes

Take this pen on your desk, for instance, or that chair by the window. Narrow your eyes until you see two pens or two chairs. Sometimes this can be done only at night or when you're quite tired. But once you see two of the object, say the chair, focus back to one, now jump to two again. Do this several times. The chair will waver, it will ripple like cards being shuffled. Do not become frightened and make the mistake of holding to the belief that a chair cannot become other than itself. Instead, flow with what you are seeing.

Let your mind accept that the chair is not a chair at all but a mere combination of light and motion that occasionally congeals into a chair then leaps apart into a frenzy of wood and fabric or ripples of dune grass from an off-shore wind.

The pattern of the upholstery swirls. It becomes the color of your iris. It becomes brown with flecks of green, of gold. It becomes light which is the sun which is the color of blood inside your brain.

And the pattern of your present chemistry changes, too, with the light, with random combinations of molecules leaping synapses, with letting go and flowing with the chair, the way it moves until there is no chair but only you asleep dreaming of one which is first of all two chairs, then several, then your grandmother's lap and she is wearing a print dress, then your grandmother's mother whom you never knew but whose eyes were hazel or sometimes brown depending on what she wore, and there were, your grandfather remembers, brilliant flecks of green, of gold.

The Sound of Wailing

There was a boy once who lived in the town of North Cumberland and who was very poor and unhappy. One day he met an old lady who gave him ten dollars. The lady told him he could spend it on whatever he wished. So he bought candy, pop, some chocolate cakes, a monster magazine.

The next day he was still unhappy. He saw the lady again and was given another ten dollars. This time the boy was practical. He bought a pair of jeans and tennis shoes. But as soon as the money was spent it was the same again. It seemed like each time he received something he became more empty.

The following day he returned to the old lady and this time he asked for and received twenty dollars. But again the same story. A silk shirt, some comic books, two movies, and it was gone. The boy was emptier than ever. He could not make anything he received truly his own. Then an idea occurred to him. He would begin saving the money. He would save each ten and twenty dollar bill he received from his generous benefactress. He did this.

As years went by he became a wealthy man. He invested his money, owned lands and businesses. Yet, he was still unhappy. Emptiness grew with each acre of land, each factory chimney. Nothing could be done for him. The more money he made, the emptier he became. One day he simply disappeared.

"I'm here!" he screamed from the smoke floating out of the factory chimneys and over the fields. "I'm here! I'm here!" But no one heard. Having given nothing away—not even himself—he had no presence in the world.

The people of North Cumberland have abandoned the factories, have let the fields lie fallow. They make love and share whatever they have. They are full and they are happy. And the sound of wailing beyond the factory chimneys, over the roofs of houses, distrubs them no more than wind among the maples, or a loon calling from across the lake.

His Father's Son

"Shall I wear my raincoat today?"

"That's your decision," the father replied. "If you think there is a chance of rain, then it would probably be wise to be prepared for that contingency. Better safe than wet I always say. If, on the other hand, it does not appear to you that it will rain, then perhaps such a precaution would be superfluous."

"Shall I kiss you goodbye on my way to school?"

"A good question," observed the father. "If you feel the need for affection, then a kiss would, I think, be proper. However, if you do not and the kiss is merely to be *pro forma*, then I think kissing under the circumstances would be inauthentic."

"There is a third possibility to be considered," noted the son.

"What might that be?" asked the father.

"It's something you'll have to decide for yourself," replied the son, kissing his father, kissing his father, kissing his father.

The Woman-on-the-Hill
And the Cabinet Maker

The cabinet maker was not very famous, but he did his work quietly and well. Each cabinet was made of white pine, carefully sawed and planed. He used screws of stainless steel, good brass hinges, and three coats of clear varnish which prevented warping. Any cabinet he made would easily outlast the kitchen in which it was installed. Or even the house where the kitchen was for that matter. He built his cabinets to last forever.

The Woman-On-The-Hill was told by a satisfied customer of the cabinet maker's about his fine work. She was quite impressed by what she heard and went directly to his shop the next day.

"Sir," she said, "I'd like a fine cabinet. I'm prepared to pay handsomely for your very best."

The cabinet maker told her: "I'll build you the finest cabinet I am capable of making. One of white pine, with screws of stainless steel, brass hinges, and three coats of clear varnish to prevent warping."

"Fine," she replied. "But I insist that you accept double payment for your work. In addition, I will tell all my neighbors and friends what a very fine cabinet maker you are.

"But that's not necessary," he told her.

"I insist," said the Woman-On-The-Hill, pressing the bills into his hand then hurrying out.

After leaving his shop, she went to the city where she praised the work of the cabinet maker to everyone she met. She created a demand for his fine product which heretofore had been little known outside his small village.

The cabinet maker had other cabinets to work on besides that ordered by the Woman-Oh-The-Hill. But within a week she was back again.

"How is my cabinet coming?" she asked.

"I've not yet begun work on it," the cabinet maker replied.

"I see," she said, pulling a sheaf of bills out of her purse and pressing them into his hand.

"It's not a question of money!" he protested.

But she left again, headed for the city where she told her friends about the very special cabinet she would have since she had paid four times the going price.

A month later she returned to the cabinet maker. The first coat of varnish had just been applied and it gleamed handsomely in the light. It was finely crafted. When the additional coats of varnish were finally applied, the screws of stainless steel tightened down, and the bronze hinges solidly mounted, it would be a cabinet which would last forever.

Next to it on the shop bench were two exact duplicates. Around the shop were a dozen others in various stages of construction.

"Who are these other cabinets for?" asked the Woman-On-The-Hill, visibly shaken, for she had expected something more than what others might receive.

"Of the completed cabinets, one is for an old teacher," he replied, "and the other is for a farmer's wife. The rest I am working on for various people outside this village."

"But they are all much like mine!" she objected.

"Each one is the very best cabinet I am capable of making," replied the cabinet maker.

"But I paid you four times the going rate for cabinets. I spread the word of your good work. Surely I should get something better than the others!"

"What would you have me do?" asked the cabinet maker. "Each cabinet I make is the very best I am capable of making. Would you have me make a bad cabinet for those who pay me less?"

"I think you're being very inconsiderate," replied the Woman-On-The-Hill.

"Then I shall give you your money back," said the cabinet maker.

"I don't want my money back, ungrateful peasant! I want a cabinet better than anyone else's!"

"Then I'm afraid," said the cabinet maker, "you've come to the wrong place. Each of my cabinets is the best that I can make."

"In that case," said the Woman-On-The-Hill, "there is only one solution."

Whereupon she picked up an ax from the corner of the room and chopped up all the cabinets in sight but one. Then she cut off the cabinet maker's hands so that he could make no more cabinets of any kind.

After leaving the shop she proceeded to destroy all the cabinets in the village. Before the week was out she had obliterated all the cabinets in the city and in the surrounding countryside as well.

When all this was done she held a tea party and invited her friends to see the only cabinet in existence made by the famous cabinet maker with no hands. But her friends laughed at her. They talked behind her back.

"Everybody knows," they said, "a man without hands cannot make a cabinet."

And the cabinet maker himself when asked, pronounced her cabinet to be a pale imitation with only a single coat of varnish, loose screws and dangling hinges.

"It will likely warp," he said, "with the first good rain."

The Message of Onan

In the Galapagos is a sea turtle who falls in love with a rock. Early in the morning he rises from the froth of the sea and mounts the rock as it lies damp and cool in the sand. He bites the igneous skin, moving his feet curiously in the air. He climaxes, then slides softly to the sand beside it.

Scientists at the Charles Darwin Institute name him Onan because he casts his seed without hope of procreation. But they are lost in the mechanics of things. For Onan the rock is Other and unity possible. For Onan his seed is not cast away but toward. His bites, the movement of his feet in the air, are yearning toward wholeness, driving for form.

At the Charles Darwin Institute they think they have it figured out. But the universe is flowing like a neap tide and they merely observe one departure. To leap before the movement, to see galaxies sleek and cool as pubescent maidens is the message of Onan, ironically named.

III : A LION
AT A COCKTAIL PARTY

The Poem

One day I had a poem in me that wouldn't come out. I lost sleep over it, grew anxious and irritable. My friends became alarmed when I ignored their questions. My wife felt shut out. I decided to fast and ate nothing for several days. Still, the poem wouldn't come out. My wife threatened to leave me. I left her instead and moved in with the dog. The dog moved out the first night. He couldn't stand my howling at the moon. The neighbors threw shoes out the window and I put the oldest pair of them on and walked to the park.

A policeman stopped me knowing I was a suspicious character: skinny, unshaven, mumbling to myself, and naked but for the old pair of shoes. He asked for identification and I had none. He asked who I was and I couldn't tell him. I told him I wasn't even wearing my own shoes. He asked me for a poem. I told him I was trying to think of one. He advised me of my rights, which were (to tell the truth) negligible. Men of no identity without even a poem, he said, are a danger to children. Besides, no decent man walks in the park without a wife or dog.

I was taken away to the jail where they told me I would be allowed to go home when I discovered who I was. But already bad things were happening. The dog died. My wife went off and joined the circus. My friends (who knew trouble when they saw it) volunteered for the Police Reserve and patroled the park at night. I wrote feverishly, turning out a hundred poems a day and passing them to the jailer when he brought the food. "No good," he told me. "We cannot accept just *any* poem. It must be the exact one you were trying to find."

Years went by. I lost whole pieces of my mind. My hair grew thin and my breathing shallow. I forgot what I was trying to remember. One night I went to sleep and dreamed the poem I had been trying to find. I wrote it out carefully on two sheets of yellow lined paper. It was exactly the poem I had been trying to get out. Still in my dream, a guard came by and took the two pieces of paper to the head jailer. "THE POEM! HE'S WRITTEN THE POEM!" the jailer announced over the P.A. system. The whole cellblock was rejoicing and the visiting nurse (who *never* smiled) was laughing!

In the morning I awoke and called for the jailer. ''What poem?'' he asked me. The cellblock was quiet. The visiting nurse asked me: did I pray for my dog, and why wasn't there an ad in the lost and found for my wife? Everyone around me began acting irritable and becoming anxious. Some started fasting, and others began losing their hair.

They have my poem and it is killing them. I could have told them that. It almost killed me.

Please Remove One
Of the Enclosed Tokens

And place it in a convenient slot. If you are interested in this offer, use the YES token. If you are not interested but would like chance at a free prize anyway, use the NO token.

I sent this offer to ten thousand women. Fifteen hundred arrived at my front door the first month. Most had YES tokens inserted neatly in their vaginas. I had to inspect them very carefully since the writing was difficult to read with all the pubic hair. Over five hundred had YES tokens in their teeth. Another five hundred had YES tokens between their buttocks.

Some of the tokens were returned by the women's husbands or lovers. One was fondling a YES token in his right hand. Another had a NO token in his left ear. He said he wanted a free prize but he didn't like dirty tricks.

I assured him that everybody had an equal chance to win.

''I'm partially deaf,'' he apologized. ''I hope I haven't offended you by putting a NO token in my ear.''

''Not at all,'' I told him. ''I respect how you feel.''

Later I told my friend, the Ear, Nose & Throat Specialist. He plied the man with drinks at a local cocktail lounge. Then he cured the man's deafness with a blunt instrument.

Applied Science #2

You pick a good psychiatrist, one whose name has appeared in the journals, whose reputation is unassailable. You are open as an oyster on the half shell, telling him everything. These sessions are important. A good report and you return to the command post assured the troops will follow.

But when the last session is over, there are strong forebodings. Days later his diagnosis arrives. The carbon has gone to company headquarters. It is too late to intercept it.

So you must think rationally. Why would he slander you? Could he be on Their side merely pretending to be one of Us? Unlikely. So, what then? He is one of the Namers who scream: *Chimeron, Lilith, Beelzebub, Lucifer,* hoping One who is named will abjectly come forth.

You are looking over your shoulder alert to any change in tone, any flickering of the light. But already disintegration has begun. You are named, pinned on a board like a species of Lepidoptera. Soon those around you, like housewives shopping for groceries, will see only the label. Other voices will fade: *Raphael, Gabriel, Michael,* silent, lost in the darkness.

Refunding
For a Therapeutic Community
—At Fort Grant, Arizona

It takes almost five minutes for a good flint drill to bore one hole in the skull. Thus, it is important the inmate have a positive attitude and really wish to be cured. He must have a year or more to serve, since several sections must be hollowed out before a yarmulke of bone is lifted off releasing the pressure.

Some inmates wander off into the desert, wild-eyed, dreaming of a place beyond the mountains. They must be brought back with dogs and deputies. For them the cure is unsuccessful.

But others wear the circle of skull like an amulet around their necks. They have discovered a house of a thousand rooms and no one lives there. Free to do whatever they wish, free to go wherever they choose. One remarks how pleasant it is to go without an erection for six months. Another, discharged for years, sweeps the warden's driveway each morning. Only a handful complain of intermittent headaches.

There is a smell of bone and flint heavy as ozone in the air. A bespectacled man is hurrying down the road acknowledging the smiles of inmates as he goes. In his briefcase there is good news from Washington.

The Gymnast

"I've known several cases of demonic possession," said the Jesuit, "and in each case there was one crack where the Devil entered. It is necessary to find that crack if one is to cast Him out."

"What do you mean by a crack, Reverend Father?" asked the theology student.

"A weakness taken for a strength, or a strength which becomes a weakness. For example, there was once a young gymnast who was so handsome and so supple that he took to having intercourse with himself. One day, having given himself over completely to this passion, the Devil arrived. The gynmast saw him coming; there was time for the gymnast to pull out, to collect himself and escape possession."

"Is there always time, Father?"

"Always, my son. But in this case, like so many others investigated by the divine office, the lad ignored the warnings. He was just about to have a climax—anticipatory and receptive—and could not repel the Devil in such an ecstasy."

"Give the Devil His due," observed the theology student.

"Indeed," replied the Jesuit, fondling the Olympic medal hidden beneath his soutane.

A Lion at a Cocktail Party

For the past fifteen minutes there has been a lion sitting in the green and blue lawn chair on the patio. He has an uncombed mane the color of wheat rotted in the field by August rain. His eyes are sleepy. His teeth yellow and stout as a hayrake. His breath stinks of carrion.

No one considers it unusual that he should be sitting here on the patio. The doctor's wife is puking into the pool. The doctor himself is taking notes for his sixteenth book.

I put my cocktail down. I light a cigarette and stare at the lion. I am a little frightened and my hand trembles. But gradually as I look at him sitting on *my* patio, in *my* lawn chair with his paw scratching the aluminum and shredding the canvas straps, I begin to get angry. Just who does he think he is? How presumptuous!

I pick up my cocktail and throw it at him. "Get the fuck off my patio, lion!"

He bares his teeth. His eyes gleam like caution lights on a darkened highway. He springs from the lawn chair and pounces upon me. His breath is heavy; his mane matted with dried blood and brain tissue. I am astounded. I had hoped to frighten him with a firm stand. Now it is clear he has seen through me.

The doctor has stopped taking notes. His wife has removed the spittle from her chin with a bath towel. They are looking in my direction, but what they see is uncertain. A pregnant woman hemorrhaging near the bar. A child who has murdered his father. Someone slipping over that fine edge, derailed finally at a cocktail party. A man eating a lion in broad daylight with two witnesses we know of.

Apostate

The man who believed in nothing, not even himself, was inconsolable. "In the end we are all sucked into the black hole," he was fond of saying, "Schweitzer and Hitler alike."

He was happiest when he confronted a believer and exposed the illogic of a cherished credo. For that reason most of those who knew him concealed their true beliefs like those timorous Romans who worshipped in catacombs.

One day he met a woman who also swore she believed in nothing. At first he was confounded. But he managed by astute examination to discover that, while the woman scorned God and the Trinity, the reality of planets and galaxies, she did believe in one thing. She believed in that which appears first as a mist beyond the trees and then grows ripe and heavy with labor. The woman measured her life by this phenomenon. She was fond of saying to her husband at dinner: "It was a fine day, my darling." Or, "I'm glad this day is over."

The man who believed in nothing explained to her that there was no such thing as a day. He showed her how the sun merely lit up the night in the same way a candle might, or a tungsten lamp. "The light goes on in London," he told her, "when it is extinguished in New York. But everywhere and always it is night, though the sun, dependable as a streetlamp, periodically illumines the darkness."

The man who believed in nothing, not even himself, saw the beginnings of doubt in the woman's eyes. But he did not press his advantage, which consisted at least in part on having none around him who clung to this position with such desperate tenacity.

2380 Market Street

When her husband died she developed a fear of open places. It happened suddenly. One morning she walked outside and the world was one great vista. Trees were flying off in space. There seemed a mile of lawn between her house and the neighbor's clothesline.

She called the grocer and was bubbly when he arrived. She gave him a large tip and hoped he would notice nothing unusual.

She felt this fear made her vulnerable. So she looked in the mirror to see if she appeared to be a different person. She rehearsed her speech to the grocer which she had already made. ''Put the box on the kitchen table and here's a dollar for your trouble. Lovely day. Lovely day. Lovely day.'' She tried this several times with different inflections.

Even the house itself seemed large and overwhelming. So she began living in one room. She slept on the kitchen table, put the t.v. on top of the refrigerator, her cosmetic case on the stove. And the days began to run together like a pack of Alaskan wolves trying to elude the light plane, the scope of a carbine.

Her skin became melba toast. Her life closed in around itself like a butter dish. No matter who telephoned, she was too busy. The neighborhood children called her The Mean Witch of Market Street.

One day some child broke her kitchen window. She flew into the child's soul. It was quiet, soft and confident. She lives there now, waiting for when the child marries, celebrates a golden anniversary, has grandchildren, loses a spouse, awakes one morning to find the world one great vista.

To a Poet on the Edge

It's hard now to recall the exact day, but you saw clouds as great puffs of chalk, or the days as galaxies, each one spiralling outward and unknowable. And every time you wrote of these things people applauded.

You thought it was something everyone had, this gift of seeing all things in terms of something else. You thought the gift might last forever even when words failed.

Then, shortly after your eighth book (the one critics praised so highly), all the words fell away. And that wasn't the worst of it. Your art presumed differences, you discovering connections. But now the trees *are* broken men, *are* old shoes, stratocumulus, the rain, the earth.

And this is a natural consequence of your art. This is where all poetry leads. And when you discover the words finally to say it, you know it is too insipid, too commonplace to publish. So the words fall away unuttered. You are constantly depressed. You lie in bed most of the day. Friends shake their heads sadly, wondering what has become of you.

There is a fly in your bedroom. He is banging against the window trying desperately to get out. Soon he'll be as wise as you.

IV : GOLDEN

The Quarry

The path behind the tennis court slopes down through heavy brush to a rock quarry which was mined out years ago. There is glass at the base of the quarry and beer cans twisted, punctured with 22's. There are weeds like the tufts of hair on a balding man, thin and sad in the afternoon sun. The two boys go there to drink wine and smoke.

There are deep rifts and crevices in the quarry. There are caves made by the blasted rock and great sections of conduit below where a child could hide. The boys opt for the high ground. They climb the ragged face of the quarry. Sixty feet up they find a deep crevice with room for both to sit or lie down in. From thie aerie, the boys see the high school off to the west; the ballfield, tennis players, the macadam basketball courts bounded on the east by Carroll Avenue. A few cars drive slowly toward the beach. The cars are small, and the people small and vulnerable.

One of the boys opens the wine and gives the other first pull. The other takes a deep one, grimaces, gulps it down past the momentary nausea, then settles back to wait for the warm belly glow of it. He lights up, and the smoke is thick, richer because of the wine. It is a good day.

From the south they hear high calls and shouts of people at the beach. The screams and laughter of young girls a mile away. The boys do not speak. They drink slowly and pass the smoke between them. They have unlimited power. Their position is unassailable. Even a howitzer would have to blast away tons of cliff before it could reach them. From the base of the rock face and from the summit the boys cannot be seen. Invisibility, the precipice, euphoria of youth and the high of a summer day convey certain powers.

Aztec priests would convey young virgins to a summit, then throw their warm and trembling bodies down the sheer Mazatlan cliffs. There were reasons for this which were not religious. Except, perhaps, in the sense that two wine-taut princes high above a New England town, strong and bronze in the afternoon sun, are religious.

They saw the virgins where they lay impaled and violated by the rocks below. They defended the heights against marauding Spaniards who had other uses for their women. Then they slept.

On the way home the two chewed young grass and mint leaves. They waved to cars passing by, returning from the beach. Adults, condescending, waved back.

Two boys in summer, swinging at the weeds by the road. Laughing, spitting green and careless in the late afternoon.

The Virgin of San Loc

In the village of San Loc lived a priest who did not believe Christ rose from the dead. Each day he said the Divine Office and Daily Mass. Each day he changed the bread and wine into the Body and Blood of Christ. That, he felt, was a credible miracle. But the miracle which in fact made the Church possible (although he never thought of it quite that way), the miracle of Christ's resurrection, he did not believe.

Easter Sunday was a difficult time for him. All the faithful in the village came to the High Mass. He would be dressed in his white robes trimmed with gold which belonged not to him but to the parish. They were hundreds of years old and dated back to when the Spanish missionaries first came to San Loc. "Hallelujah, hallelujah", the children of the parish would sing, "Ha-lay-luh-yah."

Each Sunday after the gospel was said on the left side of the altar in Latin, the priest descended the steps and walked to the pulpit to deliver his sermon. There he would castigate the peasants of the village for not attending Mass regularly, urge them to contribute to the poor or praise them for a good work. Often, he would teach them the meaning of the day's gospel. Easter Sunday was the same with this exception: on Easter, by tradition, immediately after ascending the pulpit the priest would say, "He is risen. Hallelujah!" and the peasants would answer: "Hallelujah!"

This Easter he couldn't say it. He knew that as he heard the children singing. His palms began to sweat as he walked across to the gospel side of the altar. He nodded to the altar boy who brought the book, then began reading the Latin without thinking of the words. What could he tell these people? Simple as they were in their faith, faithful as they were in their traditions, the omission of the anticipated words would trouble them and, yes, even frighten them. Yet, he could not say the words. How he agonized those last few moments as he descended the altar. Finally, as he walked slowly toward the pulpit, a solution presented itself. The sun rises and the sun sets, he thought. And God created the sun. Reassured with these thoughts, he ascended the pulpit and looked out over his flock.

"The sun of God," he said, "has risen, hallelujah!" After the briefest of pauses the peasants answered, ''Hallelujah'', and the priest began telling them of the wonder of God. As he spoke the sun entered the church through a crack in the stained glass window. It caught the edge of the crucifix on the altar, and the reflected light touched the page the priest was reading. The light touched upon one word in his notes, and the word was ''faith.'' So, the priest talked about faith, the burning bush in the desert, the fire in the hearts of martyrs, the flaming heart of Christ. And as he spoke the light moved to another word and that word was ''death''. So he told his flock of the death of sin which Christ by His death offered to the world. He spoke of the death of the soul which rotted in the body from sin and lack of faith.

As the priest talked, an angel dressed in white came down and stood beside him. He could not see the angel. No one in the congregation saw the angel, either, except a little girl. She saw the angel raise a burning sword, she saw the white vestments of the priest turn black, she cried out: ''Die! Faithless priest!'' and immediately the angel left. The priest crumpled to a heap at the bottom of the pulpit. His skin turned black as if he had been dead for weeks. A horrible stench rose up from the rotting body. The congregation, following the example of the little girl, filed past the body, each member spitting as he passed, and the sound of the spit striking the face of the priest was the sound of water splattering on a hot skillet.

For years the sun did not come to San Loc. The skies were always gray, winds blew the dust in ugly swirls across the narrow streets. The little girl grew older and disappeared from the village and the people grew sick and aged. The church spire crumbled and the birds departed. No flowers grew in the gardens.

The people of San Loc no longer believed in miracles. They began worshippinng the spirit that lived in the peyote button and sang ancient songs to the moon. They danced at night in mad, whirling steps. They were known as the Lost People, and no one could save them except the little girl who left the village.

The little girl was taken in at a Mexico City brothel at the age of twelve. She was much in demand, being blonde, petite and innocent. Her first customer was a man dressed in white with a flaming sword. He lifted her dress and spread her legs. She screamed as the sword ripped through her loins, and the birds in the city flew away in fright.

The birds flew north where they settled in the abandoned village of San Loc. Many came to rest in the deserted churchyard. The next day the sun came to the village. A new priest arrived shortly thereafter. Children were born and a new steeple erected. Flowers grew in the garden and the people once again believed in miracles.

A Nursing Mother on the
Dorchester-Harvard Train

It's good to leave the South End if only for a day. Good to trust where the tracks lead as your child does that dark areole. To forget there's not nearly enough nectar for the rich combs of honey his dreaming takes.

At the Park Street Station you offer the other breast. You guide it like Soyuz into Apollo. Above you the sign says: *Double Your Freshness, Double Your Fun.*

You are going to the clinic, perhaps? There is little else for you this side of the river. Each time you arrive you discover you have none of the tokens to linger here.

I imagine the child screaming over the high-pitched steel as the subway returns to Dorchester . . . Roxbury. What will you offer him then? Your breasts pleated like empty wineskins. A finger soaked in amber liquid? Your dreams? Listen. A chewing gum jingle? The rhythmic rocking of the train?

A Question of Time

"You will always have trouble being understood no matter how clearly you speak," said Mrs. Murphy, the drama coach.

"Why is that?" I asked.

"It's a question of tone. Take the dial tone, for example. A steady murmur means the line is unoccupied. A high-pitched whine means you've got the wrong number. With you a person never knows where he stands."

"Perhaps he should sit then until he figures it out."

"Perhaps you should sit and do the exercises again. Remember the tone is a important as the words. Do not grin foolishly when saying 'FUCK YOU!' Do not crinkle your nose seductively when telling your teacher 'good morning.' Do not sound like you are making an indecent proposal each time you ask to go to the bathroom."

"Okay," I said and buckled down to the exercises. I imitated the dial tone for thirty minutes, then the high-pitched squeal for over an hour.

When Mrs. Murphy returned, she sat down beside me.

"Have you learned anything by practicing the exercises?"

"I think so," I replied.

"Fine. Then repeat after me: 'May I please go to the bathroom, Mrs. Murphy?'"

"May I please go . . ." I began, but it was too late. She was already out of her panties, her hand caressing my leg.

A Name

The word "tiger" is a powerful word, muscular, even deadly. And this has nothing at all to do with any particular jungle cat. There was the tiger tank, for example. Also a boxer who moved quickly with a feline grace and what they call "killer instinct."

Were someone to say, *don't use the word "tiger" anymore, use "mozab" instead*, I would object. A man-eating mozab is nebulous as an amoeba. Any self-respecting village would be ashamed to have one lurking about.

Words are important. And certain family names are magical. Mine is that of an Irish clan which fought the Romans, Danes, and Saxon chiefs. It was a name whispered in fear by English infantry crossing the Boyne. A name shouted in the streets during the Revolution when the Dublin postoffice burned.

My grandfather gave me more than a few Celtic words and a secret handshake. Before he died, he connected me with kings and warriors, with poets and arrogant barristers. A green island of songs and long days, my boyo. A land that had universities when all of Europe still swung by their tails from trees. That's all in our name, bucko, and smiles that light up the darkest room."

So I tell my son, "Don't change your name as your mother has."

"I'd never do that," he vows. "It's the name of my first father."

I question him closely to determine if first father (who is me) is like First Secretary of the Communist Party or like *The* Father in Rome. It is too much of one, too little of the other to let it rest. So I teach him the Celtic handshake. Recite the ancient Gaelic words. Speak to the green island his blood knows, singing deep in his veins.

Water, Water

I read it somewhere. More people die in the desert from drowning than of thirst. One of those statements so delightfully incongruous you know it's true.

In August the monsoon comes like a rhinoceros, unwieldy, recklessly inconsiderate. It is muddy and unkempt. A raft capsizes on the Colorado flushing red-faced men and beer cans into the California Gulf.

On the Gila, a father who can't swim dies to save his children who can't swim. Mothers stand on canal banks waiting for the bodies of infants caught in a fireman's hook like carp.

Somewhere, perhaps a mile to the south, a man is dying of thirst.

And two hobos camped in a dry wash near the Catalinas hear a roar one August night, like a diesel cruising down the expressway, or a locomotive passing the Union Pacific yards. Each takes a pull at the wine bottle, then returns to sleep. And the flash flood takes them in their sleep like a warm brown hand and carries them west to a lineman's shack where they are found the next morning.

In August saguaros grow fat as pregnant ladies. Spadefoot toads make love in sequestered pools. The desert is alive and moving. And a coyote pleads with the moon.

The Overnight

First you pretend to have forgotten your sleeping bag back at the camp. You approach hers. You are shivering in the night air, helpless as a coyote in the sheepfold.

"I forgot my sleeping bag," you tell her. "May I crawl in with you just to get warm?"

"Definitely not," she tells you.

But you look so helpless, so damned uncomfortable, she lets you lie on top of her sleeping bag so that you'll at least be off the cold ground.

You begin shivering. You shiver a lot below the waist until your penis gets as hard as a railroad spike.

"My goodness!" she says. "If you're that cold you might as well crawl inside."

During the night a counselor hears the bleat of a lamb. It is a desperate sound. Violent and sensual.

The Magician

The magician is trying to fathom a mystery. How many rabbits might come from a broken egg in a fedora borrowed from a man in the front row? People say: How does he do it? The truth is, he doesn't quite know.

A magician can teach technique. He can show you how to move your hands (which are quicker than, etc.), how to ruffle the cape. But this is not magic. This is merely the trick. This is getting you to look for something other than what is about to appear. This is how father delights the children at Christmas. He leads them to expect a piece of coal, then produces a Golden Retriever. That's the trick. If you've dealt with children, you hardly underestimate the degree of duplicity required.

Good parents are liars like good magicians. And something more. The retriever came from a store where it was bought with father's beer money. But where did the child come from? The rabbits? The movement of the father away from his evening sixpack toward the Golden Retriever? The softness of the mother's laugh? The retriever himself trusting the father, the mother, the children?

It is the business of the magician to discover these things, to become the father, to live inside the retriever, experience the promiscuity of rabbits. The question to be asked always is not how he does it, but why. And the answer, another question.

Golden

Fifty years. The children light fifty candles on the cake. The grandchildren stand in a circle around the grandfather.

"Blow out the candles!" they cry.

Grandfather begins to blow out the candles. He blows hard and ten candles go out. He inhales. The flames from the other candles lick back across the cake and re-light the ten he blew out.

"Happy Anniversary!" the children shout.

Grandmother looks worried. But Grandfather smiles and blows on the cake harder this time. He gets twenty-two candles with one sustained exhalation. He inhales, and most of them are re-kindled.

"Blow faster, Grandfather!" the children cry. They are laughing and dancing around the cake. Grandmother looks worried. She tries to smile, but is not successful. Grandfather's face is red. Beads of perspiration pop out on his upper lip, his forehead. He is blowing harder, faster. A vein in his temple is throbbing. But he makes no headway on the candles.

"Do not stop for a breath, Grandfather! You can do it!"

Grandfather's hands have turned blue. He is clutching his chest. He collapses on the floor. The vein in his temple no longer throbs. Most of the candles are still burning.

The children gather about Grandmother. She is crying, and they try to console her. But the grandchildren pull at her dress.

"Come on, Grandmother!" they shout. "We cannot eat the cake until *someone* blows out the candles."

Other Works by Michael Hogan:

POETRY
LETTERS FOR MY SON (Unicorn Press, 1975)
IF YOU EVER GET THERE, THINK OF ME (Emerald City Press, 1975).
SOON IT WILL BE MORNING (Cold Mountain Press, 1976).
RUST (Turkey Press, 1977).

PROSE
A LION AT A COCKTAIL PARTY (Gallimaufry Press, 1978).

TAPES
APRIL, 1976 (Cold Mountain Press, 1976), a 120 minute cassette.

ANTHOLOGIES
DO NOT GO GENTLE (Blue Moon Press, 1977).

Michael Hogan was born in Newport, Rhode Island in 1943. He is a freelance writer and reviewer, and the associate editor of Cold Mountain Press in Austin, Texas.

He has worked as a law clerk, a teacher of retarded children, a tutor of Romance languages, and as a civil liberties advocate and legal technical assistant.

He has written five collections of poetry, and his essays and short stories have appeared in numerous magazines and anthologies. He received a 1975 P.E.N. Award, a 1976 Joseph Fels Award, and a 1976-1977 fellowship from the National Endowment for the Arts.

Presently he is living in Tucson, Arizon with his son, Gary, and a cat, a dog and seven guinea pigs.

A LION AT A COCKTAIL PARTY
is printed in a limited second edition of five hundred,
twenty-six of which are lettered and signed by the author.
This is copy _____.

Typeset in twelve point Holland Seminar.
Designed by Mary MacArthur.
Cover design from a drawing by Shari McCoul.
Printed at the West Coast Print Center.

1978